GOODBYE HOUSE

FRANK ASCH

Simon and Schuster Books for Young Readers
Published by Simon & Schuster Inc., New York

SIMON AND SCHUSTER BOOKS
FOR YOUNG READERS
Simon & Schuster Building
Rockefeller Center
1230 Avenue of the Americas
New York, New York 10020
SIMON AND SCHUSTER BOOKS FOR YOUNG READERS
is a trademark of Simon & Schuster Inc.
Manufactured in Spain

10 9 8 7 6 5 4 3 2
10 9 8 7 6 5 4 3 2 1 (pbk)

Library of Congress Cataloging-in-Publication Data
Asch, Frank.   Goodbye, house.
Summary: Just before leaving with his family for the
move to their new home, Little Bear says goodbye to all
his favorite places in and around his old house.
[1. Moving, Household—Fiction. 2. Dwellings—
Fiction. 3. Bears—Fiction] I. Title.
PZ7.A778God   1986   [E]   85-19263
ISBN-0-671-67054-9
ISBN-0-671-67927-9 pbk

To Randy, Debbie, Serena, Emily,
Richie, and Phoebe Moon

When all the furniture was packed
in the moving van, Baby Bear said,
"Wait a minute. I think I forgot something,"
and he ran inside.

First he looked in the dining room and the
kitchen. He looked in the living room, the bathroom,
and in all of the bedrooms. Then he looked in the
attic and the cellar. He looked everywhere.

But the house was empty.

"Did you find what you were looking for?" asked
Mama Bear.

"No, Mama," said Baby Bear, "the house is empty."

"So you think the house is empty," said Papa Bear.

"Yes," said Baby Bear with a sigh,

"everything we own is in the van."

"What about the memories?" said Papa Bear.

"I remember where my chair used to go," said Mama.

"My chair was right there," said Papa Bear.

"And mine was right here," said Baby Bear.

For a moment everything in the house looked just

as it was before, but soon...

...it all...

. . . faded away.

"Come on," said Papa Bear, "let's say goodbye."
And he picked up Baby Bear
and carried him from room to room.

They said goodbye to the dining room...

and the stairs.

They said goodbye to the bedrooms and the halls,

the ceilings and the walls.

They said goodbye to the attic...

...and the cellar.

They said goodbye to the floors, the doors,
the windows, and the kitchen sink.
And when they had said goodbye to
everything in the back yard...

they locked the front door...

and said goodbye to the whole house.

Then they climbed into the moving van

and drove away.

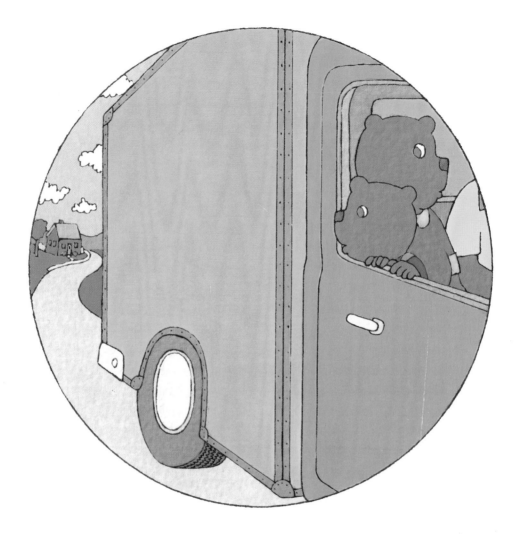

And as they drove away, Baby Bear said,
"That's what I forgot.
I forgot to say goodbye."

BAKER & TAYLOR